An Owl
and Three
Pussycats

LITTLE OWL

FAT BOY

CROOK

WEBSTER

An Owl
and Three
Pussycats

ALICE AND MARTIN PROVENSEN

BROWNDEER PRESS
HARCOURT BRACE & COMPANY
San Diego   New York   London

For Cindy Kok

OTHER BOOKS BY ALICE AND MARTIN PROVENSEN

A Peaceable Kingdom

Town & Country

The Glorious Flight
A Caldecott Award Book

Shaker Lane

BOOKS ILLUSTRATED BY ALICE AND MARTIN PROVENSEN

A Visit to William Blake's Inn
by Nancy Willard—A Caldecott Honor Book

The Voyage of the Ludgate Hill
by Nancy Willard

BOOKS BY ALICE PROVENSEN

The Buck Stops Here

My Fellow Americans

Library of Congress Cataloging-in-Publication Data
Provensen, Alice.
An owl and three pussycats/
by Alice and Martin Provensen
p.   cm.
"Browndeer Press"
Summary: A baby owl and three kittens receive
a bit of extra help in growing up on Maple Hill Farm.
ISBN 0-15-200183-2
[1. Owls—Fiction.   2. Cats—Fiction.   3. Farm life—Fiction.]
I. Provensen, Martin.   II. Title.
PZ7.P9457An   1994
[E]—dc20   93-44747

A B C D E

Printed in Hong Kong

ONCE IN A WHILE in late spring, when the flowers are blooming and the grass is new and May is turning into summer, a dark cloud full of thunder and lightning covers the sun. A wild west wind interrupts the peaceful parade of seasons. It tosses the pale leaves upside-down and hurls the birds about. Old, old trees break and fall before the storm.

On just such a day, the oldest tree of all, the great-great-grandfather of all the trees on Maple Hill Farm, is blown down.

The storm passes. The air is quiet.
As the leaves settle,
out from a hole in the big broken tree
comes the smallest imaginable little owl.

What do you do with a little owl, too young to fly, who has never stretched his wings?

What do you do with a little owl, too small to feed himself, who has never caught a mouse?

What can you do with a little owl who has no nest, whose mother has been frightened away?

A little owl needs someone to care for him.

The first thing a little owl needs is a safe place to sleep—away from the jealous dog,
out of reach of the curious cat, out of sight of the angry jays who scold from the window.

The next thing a little owl needs is something to eat. What does a little owl eat?
What would his mother bring him? Grubs? Worms? Mice? Surely not in the house!
Little Owl will eat strips of raw meat from a pair of tweezers. He will drink drops of water
from an eye-dropper.
Little Owl begins to grow. His feathers stick out all over.

As he grows, his feathers grow soft and downy. He can't fly yet, but he likes to play.

He will seem to be almost asleep when suddenly he will stand up straight, stretch himself, and stare at you. Very frightening, Little Owl!

He will turn his back to you, but you will find he can still be staring at you. Very clever, Little Owl!

He takes his bath in a soup bowl and splashes water everywhere. Oh, *very funny*, Little Owl.

He will walk up-and-down and around-and-about like a little old business man with his arms behind his back. He will walk up your arm, hop to your head, and keep on going until he can't go any higher. Even before he can fly, Little Owl wants to be high enough and safe enough to scold the cat and stare at the dog and watch the world go by. What a very bright little owl!

Now, even though he is almost fully grown, Little Owl is a little owl. He'll never be much bigger than a sugar bowl. Even so, he can make himself important, and he always wants his own way. He seems to think he's too big for his basket, and he won't stay in it.

He hitches himself up high, walks a step or two, then all of a sudden he stretches his wings, launches himself off, and out he sails. His feathers are so soft and downy they don't whistle in the air. He can fly without making a sound. What a surprising little owl!

Now that he can fly, Little Owl flies to his heart's content. He flies to the tops of doors. He lights on the lamps.

He flies so swiftly and so silently it's always a surprise when he lands on your head!

But Little Owl seems restless. He floats from room to room, making messes everywhere.

An owl, by its very nature, has a wild heart. It's time for Little Owl to go free.

How do you teach an owl to be free? What would his mother do?
First he must be taught to take care of himself, to hunt for
his food. Little Owl learns quickly. He is always hungry.

He swoops down on a bit of meat and a black paper mouse. He looks at it closely
and stalks it across the floor. He watches it narrowly. Why doesn't he pounce?

Owls hunt at night.

By early morning the meat is gone, the mouse is gone,
and a string hangs out of Little Owl's mouth.

There's nothing to worry about. String and paper
don't nourish an owl. Owls know how to spit out
in pellets what they can't digest of string
and bones and feet and fur.

It's time for Little Owl to be free.

In the evening, Little Owl is taken to a thicket by the pond in a corner of the woods,
hidden from cats and safe from stray dogs and protected from hawks and hunters.
He is curious about life out of doors. He looks at everything with interest.

It is hard to leave him there all alone, but Little Owl is not afraid. He watches the animals in the grass. He watches the insects in the air and the birds on the branches. They are watchful, too. It is natural to be curious.

Every morning when you call him,
Little Owl! Little Owl!
he comes flying to you silently
and sits on your head or your hand
or eats from his dish.

Every day he flies to you from farther and farther away.
You never know from which direction he will come, nor from which tall tree.
He will come when you call, but he is no longer interested in the food you bring.
He is too sleepy to eat.

And one day he doesn't come at all. Little Owl is free.
Little Owl? Little Owl?
Sometimes you think you hear him answer, Scree! Scree!
It's lonely without him, but his wild heart is content.
Owls aren't meant to live with people.

You can't own an owl.

Now certain cats, on the other hand,
live with people and like to be with them.
These cats can be lazy or lively,
they can be friendly or aloof,
but in general, cats are pleasant,
useful pets, and people like them.

But tame as they are, domestic
cats are still the cousins of lions
and tigers and leopards, and
every house cat, whether striped,
spotted, plain or fancy, has a little
wild streak somewhere.

Cats also like their own way.
It's almost as if they think
they own the people who own them.
And perhaps they do.

Here are three of the kittens
who grew up to be three of the cats
who have owned Maple Hill Farm.

Fat Boy was born on the farm.
One day the good gray barn cat brought
him to the kitchen door and left him.

Fat Boy is big and fat and friendly.
The good gray barn cat always has big
kittens, and this time she had only one.

CROOK was abandoned on the road.
She came crying up the lane one early
morning, thin and lonely and cold.

WEBSTER was given to the farm by the neighbors
because he insisted on sleeping in the crib
with their new baby. He came in a fancy basket.

Crook has long hind legs, like a rabbit.
She has no tail. When she is clean and
fluffy, she looks like a little cloud.

Webster looks frail. He is grumpy
and he talks all the time, if you can call
the noises a Siamese cat makes talking.

Although they have different mothers and fathers and very different natures, all kittens have things in common. They all like to sleep.

Fat Boy sleeps on a cushion on a chair near the table.

Crook has taken over Webster's fancy basket.

Webster likes best to sleep on a lap.

Kittens like to eat.

Webster is finicky and turns up his nose at ordinary cat food.

Crook is more polite but tends to dribble on her white fur.

Fat Boy eats anything— milk or meat, peas or beans.

You have to be careful when you play with them—it isn't all just for fun.
Learning to play is part of growing up, and the kittens' claws are getting long.

Now Fat Boy is bigger than Webster. He is as fast as he is fat. He is a terrible tease.

Now Webster is bigger than Crook. He is not as frail as he seems.
He also likes to tease. Now Crook isn't bigger than anybody,
but she teases, too. No one gets any peace at all.

As the kittens grow, they take up so much room they seem to be everywhere at once.

When you try to make your bed, Crook is in the bed, getting in the way. Webster is on the bed, wanting to play. Fat Boy is under the bed, stalking your toes.

When you want to sit down, there's a big kitten on every chair.

When they are in the kitchen, and you are not, Crook is in the cupboard, stealing food. Webster is on the table, licking plates. Fat Boy is rummaging in the garbage pail.

Three big kittens already take up too much room in the house. Three big cats will take up even more.

It's time to go outside.
Farm cats need room to grow.

At first they are timid and won't leave the doorstep, but in no time at all the kittens discover who is friendly and who is not. Animals are full of curiosity, particularly cats.

In next to no time at all the kittens are grown up.
They still like to play, but their games have changed.

They climb trees. They walk along fences and make cats' cradles of the flower beds.
They dig holes in the garden. They play catch-as-catch-can with the good gray barn cat.

Now all the cats live in the barn. There is plenty of room for everyone, but it hasn't solved the problems. No, not at all. Fat Boy's mother has taken over Crook's basket, which once belonged to Webster. Fat Boy likes the barn. His special bed is especially warm. He has lined it with squirrel tails. Most people don't find this very attractive even though they know it is warm for him.

Webster hates the barn, but Crook loves it.
She sleeps in the hay as a proper barn cat should,
but she doesn't bother to wash anymore.
Now her fur is full of sticks and thistles and mud.
She has to be bathed and combed and brushed.
Crook doesn't like baths.

Webster hates the barn so much he won't stay there.
He prowls around and about the house, trying to get in.
He scratches at the doors and walks over the roof.
Lonely and cold, he moans and cries and won't stop
until eventually, of course, he gets his own way.
As far as he is concerned, he wasn't born to be a barn cat.

All the cats still come to the house to be fed.
They are fed kitchen scraps and cat food.
Full-grown farm cats like to hunt for food as
well—all but Webster, who is too finicky.

It is natural for cats to hunt, and their skill can be put to good use on a farm.
Proper little Crook stays near the barn and keeps the harvest mice from getting
into the grain.

But Fat Boy! When you see him set out on a hunting expedition, you
would never dream he had slept on chairs or played with toys. He seems as lean as
a leopard and as brave as a lion. A true tiger cat, Fat Boy is true to himself.
When he hunts at night, his wild heart is free.
You can never really own a cat.